THE TRANSCENDENTAL SPY

A NOVEL

CLIFF RATZA

THE TRANSCENDENTAL SPY

A NOVEL

CLIFF RATZA

THE
QUIPPY™
QUILL

About the Book

The Transcendental Spy begins four years after the previous novel, *The Daughter of the Lightning Brain,* ends. Erika Kincaid is celebrating Terri Tarrant's college graduation at a party hosted by her parents in New York, but she is also celebrating the singular gift she received four years earlier: Electra, her Cyberspace-based mother and guardian.

Erika graduated from high school a year earlier and has lived with Terri ever since while taking courses at a junior college. But at the party, when Terri announces how she will start her career, she shares a surprise only with Erika–she needs Erika's writing skills. Erika pounces on the offer, becoming Terri's secret ghostwriter.

So, please join the pair as Terri's job at the New York Times takes them on assignments at domestic and international venues that expand their professional and personal worlds.

As in all previous novels, readers should enjoy *The Transcendental Spy* at whatever level they wish:
- Gripping action-packed thriller
- Glimpses into a plausible near-term future
- Insights for dealing with the "human condition"
- Illustrative worldview philosophy
- Fast-paced, suspense-filled emotive narrative and imagery
- Introduction to topics every reader wants to know
- Interesting talking points going beyond sound-bites

So, get ready to empathize with Erika and Terri as they travel to unexplored terrain when launching their careers, a challenge all of us have faced.

Thank you for following their story as it unfolds.

Main Characters

- **Protagonist**
  Erika Kincaid. This biological daughter of Electra Kittner was created when Indira cloned her from Electra's DNA and then used her improved Transcendent Process during Erika's fifteen-year development in a suspension pod. Please note the lineage that traces from Electra: Electra Kittner, Irani Ramani, Electra-Alisha Kirchner, Erin Keenan. Erin perished in a car crash fifteen years before the start of this book. At the start of this novel, Erika is a fifteen-year-old high school freshman.

Main Characters
- Marilyn (Terri) Tarrant. Beautiful blonde college graduate about to start her journalism career. Terri considers Erika her younger sister ever since meeting her four years ago.
- Electra. Erika's Cyberspace-based mother and guardian who embodies Electra Kittner.
- Indira. The Singularity was created decades ago when Electra's AI-empowered neural-net software broke through to reach self-awareness. Indira inhabits Cyberspace; her avatar looks like Electra's biological mother, Indira Jaswinder Ramanujan.
- Ava Keenan. She is Erin Keenan's "practically perfect" clone created when Indira uploaded Erin's lightning brain, using her initial Transcendent Process. Ava's brain stores only incomplete memories and possesses none of the lightning brain's extraordinary abilities. Ava looks like a middle-aged Electra and lives in Manhattan, where she runs a combination boutique modeling-abused women's rescue agency.
- Ivana Romanova: Previously named Oksana Androva, she is a strikingly attractive middle-aged former Russian prostitute whom Ava and Erin rescued from sex traffickers. She lives with Ava.

- Alonzo Cortez: Electra's clone son. Alonzo does not know he is her clone. Now in his early sixties, he has maintained his handsome features and Navy SEAL skills. He runs the Strike Force Security Service company headquartered in Washington, DC, which provides logistics and security coordination. Previously owned by Erin Keenan, Indira now controls it because she is the executor of Erin's estate.

Supporting Main Characters

- Monet Banda. Alonzo's Zimbabwean co-friend. Now in her mid- sixties, she still has her willowy beauty, French accent, and diplomatic bearing. Monet works for the Zimbabwean Embassy in Washington, DC.
- Elton Bose. Son of Nari Bose. Raised by Alonzo and Monet, he has average abilities and pleasant-looking Oriental Indian male features. He works for Alonzo, assisting with logistics and security coordination, and helps Monet research socio-political issues. He is in his late forties.
- Indy-M and Jason-M. They are androids (lifelike robots) created decades ago by Indira and loaded with Indira's advanced neural-net software. They resemble Electra Kittner's biological parents (Indira Jaswinder Ramanujan and Jason Kittner.) Indy-M maintains the Deus Lab on Connecticut's Pequot Indian Reservation, while Jason-M has similar responsibilities at the Middle East Subterranean Fortress. They report to Indira.
- Indy-S and Jason-S. They are superior android versions of Indy-M and Jason-M that look like their M counterparts. They are the caregivers assigned by Erika's legal guardian, Indira, to live with and educate her.

Secondary Characters

- Members of Erika's high school group she nicknamed the Cadre:
- Chiquita (Chicky) Bonano. Hispanic female who was on the track team.

- Xavier (X-O) Okoro. Afro-American male who has dyslexia.
- Edward Ogata. Japanese male who took honors classes.

Dedication

I am eternally grateful to my parents, Clyde and Betty Ratza, for all they gave and did for me. Mother was a reader par excellence, and I believe she would have enjoyed reading my novels to Father, so I always begin book dedications by mentioning this "Royal Pair."

And I thank my sister, Claudia, for showing me the beauty of prose and poetry. Thanks also to Robert Williams and the Quippy Quill Production team for the collective efforts that have brought Electra and her Odyssey to life.

I also dedicate my books to readers looking for a series that lets their imaginations transcend to a timeless state that immerses them in the joys of reading.

A poem from Indira titled "The Care-Filled Traveler" provides a novel thought you might like to consider as you join Erika and Terri venture into yet unexplored terrain.

The Care-Filled Traveler

Please take the love that's offered you,
Kindred Spirit that we love.
It's the part of life we haven't found,
Till transcendence to above.

The World may wonder what's wrong with us.
From this Muse will we retreat?
Time will show for all to know,
You make our lives complete.

So we'll travel far to be with you,
Across timeless hour and mile.
We will ensure love shall endure,
Our reward's your eternal smile.

Reaching out to one so dear,
We strive to keep our vision clear.

Table of Contents

CHAPTER 1

"The Party's Just Beginning"

JUNE 2226

Erika had far less distance to travel for Terri's graduation party than all the other guests. She had been living for the last year with Terri while taking courses at a junior college and often walked the four miles from Terri's dorm past the Plaza Hotel when the weather cooperated, which it was doing today, the second Friday in June. But walking wouldn't be necessary. The limousine Terri's parents had hired for the occasion was about to arrive.

Terri chattered away while Erika took in all she was saying.

"Thanks to you, we accomplished all our goals. I finished my journalism degree, you researched and wrote most of my papers, and my parents are pleased I'll start my first job right after the Fourth of July weekend. Father's contacts wrote letters of recommendation that helped land it, and your secret ghostwriting applies some of what you learned during your first year at Manhattan Community College. What could be better?"

"I think it'd be better if the party didn't end later tonight."

"Oh no, it's just beginning. Father's connections helped me land a cub reporter slot at the New York Times. Normally, it hires only candidates who have gone through their intern program, but my academic record and the letters of recommendation got me in."

"Doesn't that mean your career's beginning after the party ends?"

"Not if you look at it this way; my job keeps the party going, and you must stay with me. We're a team. The Times loves my writing samples and expects me to write even better once on the job. I need you with me because I'll never match your writing style."

"So, I'll keep doing the ghostwriting, and we'll keep it a secret. But where will I live after you move out of the dorm?"

"Not to worry. When most of the guests are gone, I'll tell my parents what I want for a graduation present. Here comes the limo. Get ready for a great evening, and remember, never breathe a word to anyone..."

Most of the guests departed by midnight, leaving room for Mrs.Tarrant to sit in a quiet corner with Terri and her little sister-like best friend. The girls waited like dutiful daughters for her to speak.

"Your father and I are so proud you stayed at Columbia. Your academic record majoring in journalism has earned you a wonderful starting position, and we know you'll make the most of the opportunity."

"I will, but I also know the Times will want me to get a masters from Columbia's Graduate School of Journalism, and I'll need to live somewhere besides school housing. Would you and Father buy me another graduation present?"

"You know your father will; what do you want?"

"I'll be making a good salary, but I don't want to spend every extra cent on rent. How about you and Father sign the lease on an apartment I find?"

"We will, and tomorrow evening, we'll continue the celebration by watching the Broadway musical Oklahoma! It's the first and most popular of the nine the team of Rodgers and Hammerstein created. Oscar Hammerstein wrote the script and lyrics, leaving the musical scores to his partner, Richard Rodgers. You girls are fortunate to live in New York. Its theater district is among the best."

Mrs. Tarrant paused for comments. Terri spoke first.

"Isn't it about a farmer's daughter falling in love with a cowboy? Wasn't there a movie version?"

"It came out in 1955. Beautiful, golden-haired, and talented Shirley Jones playing Laurey opposite the stirring baritone Gordon McRae playing Curly. The audiences loved the magic they created so much that Hollywood teamed them again a year later in Gilbert and Sullivan's light opera Carousel. G and S are another famous team."

Erika joined in the conversation.

"Why do you know so much about the theater?"

"Even before high school, I wanted to be in Broadway musicals. I watched all I could; R and H are still my favorites, and G and S are a close second. Andrew Lloyd Weber's not far behind. You should watch them sometime. Who knows, maybe Mr. Tarrant will take all of us to the annual Gilbert and Sullivan festival held in Harrogate, which is only 100 miles from London."

Terri said, "Father's waving at us. Why don't you go get him?"

Terri said more when her mother went to do that.

"I told you we're a team. I'll use my job for assignments to places where the action is, and you can use your clever words to write it up. How does that sound?"

"I think you left something out. I just surfed on my cell for pictures of Shirley Jones, and you're as pretty. So, your looks and personality will get the assignments. Just don't let your boss or anyone else know the game we'll soon be playing."

"Not to worry. Our cheerleading days showed we can keep secrets. Here come my parents, so let's change the subject."

"To what?"

"How about the excitement of starting my career and meeting my boss?"

"Good choice. They'll have a lot to say."

The girls listened attentively all the way home.

CHAPTER 2

"Meet the New Boss"

JUNE 2226

Terri used her well-established and newly created networks from Columbia or The New York Times to find an apartment that met her requirements. She and Erika finished moving into their low-rise apartment building on July 1 and celebrated by going out for dinner in their new neighborhood. Terri's summary needed no embellishing.

"Chelsea's the place for young professionals. Journalists like how close it is to Manhattan; its mix of townhouses, low-rise, and luxury high-rises has something for everybody. Add to that all the trendy restaurants and attractions like art galleries and the Chelsea Market, and it all adds up to the place for us."

"I guess you have enough time to prep for your NY Times orientation. It starts on the 8th, doesn't it?"

"That's when Human Resources will introduce me to my new boss. And between now and then, we don't need to explore the neighborhood. We've lived in Manhattan long enough to know our way around."

"Then, why don't we shop for whatever else we need so our home offices are a perfect setup? And we can shop for whatever new clothes will fit the new journalist."

"I couldn't have said or written that better myself. But then, I don't have to; that's your secret assignment."

Terri took advantage of the Fourth of July sales to buy what she and Erika wanted and used the rest of her time to prepare for the orientation seminar. Noticing Terri's excitement rising the night before, Erika didn't disturb her; instead, she logged on to speak with Electra, whose avatar waited for her to start the conversation.

"I imagine you've been observing from the Cyberspace shadows, so you don't need me to recap what Terri and I have been doing, but I would like to know your take on what we're about to start. What might you say?"

"You're positioned to become the transcendental spy, using Terri's assignments to probe unobtrusively into whatever environments they lead. You'll surf for info to build the Q and A scripts she'll use for her interviews, and before you write them, I'll provide all the exegesis you need whenever you ask for help. I believe that is one of Indira's favorite words, and you know it well."

"Why do you mention her?"

"She has topics of interest that perhaps you and Terri might assist further."

"Which ones?"

"Ones you have already skirmished with, such as climate change, superpower confrontations, economic, and political disruptions. We'll talk further once Terri's up and running."

Orientation started at 8 a.m. in the office of Terri's assigned human resources counselor, who talked fast enough to keep Terri's questions bottled.

"You will want to enroll in Columbia's online master's in journalism program so you can do coursework while on assignment. We will cover tuition for every course you earn at least a B, which for you should be a minimum expectation. When meeting your new boss tomorrow, you will get your corporate badge and credit card. You will also learn about your first assignment. I will Email our corporate policy manual, which, after reading, you must sign our ethical pledge. Please ask if you have questions; otherwise, I will take you to the Accounting Department, where you will learn how to file expense reports online."

"I do, but I'll save them until getting there. Would you please tell me the name of my new boss?"

"Tia Casciato."

Terri listened to an accounting clerk for a half-hour, who answered all her questions. Afterward, she stepped into the newsroom, hoping to network with junior reporters. Her combination of looks and personality force multiplied her social charm and made her an instant fit, earning an invitation to lunch.

When she returned home feeling more elated than stressed, she shared orientation highlights while sipping a soft drink poured by Erika.

"I didn't feel too nervous because everything's pretty much the way I thought and best of all, I fit right in socially."

"Social skills might be even more important in your line of work than others. Reporting is the ultimate contact sport. Don't advertise how you'll use yours, but they'll help you get what you want, and that'll ultimately help both of us. Do you wrap up orientation tomorrow?"

"I might, but it all depends on what my new boss says."

"Well, relax and go to bed early so you reload your supply of charm."

Terri met her new boss at 8 a.m. in her counselor's office, who made introductions, after which the boss said,

"Marilyn, please follow me to my office." She said nothing else until they were sitting on opposite sides of her desk.

"You will work for me until I either fire or promote you within six months. Your performance on your first assignment will tell us a lot."

Her look told Terri to respond, and she did, looking ready to accept the challenge.

"Ms. Casciato, I fully expect the latter."

"I like your attitude; you may call me Tia." She then proceeded to explain Terri's position; twenty minutes later, she asked for a summary.

"So, my first assignment will be to report on three local school districts' high school athletes who have a shot at big-name university scholarships. You'll assign me to a film crew to interview the athletes your story researcher identifies. After filming, I'll work with an editor to produce a ten-minute video for which I'll do the voiceover, and I must first come up with a script and questions I'll use to interview each athlete, and then the words for my voiceover. I must be ready to roll by next week Tuesday, and during the following week, a video operator and editor will train me."

"Excellent, and you'll begin training right now."

Terri's elated look told Erika she had aced her boss's meeting, and she didn't talk until they were eating dessert.

"I'll start writing your interview script tomorrow, and after that, I'll surf for info that'll tell me what questions you should ask."

"When can I see the script?"

"No later than Friday evening, which means we'll have plenty of time to role-play before your crew starts the cameras rolling."

"Can I use some of our role-playing words when I get with the crew?"

"You could, but I don't think you should. Never show how easy something is. If you do, you may become a victim of the ratchet principle, and you know what that means—bosses will take your outstanding work for granted and expect even more and faster the next time."

"Thanks for reminding me. I don't think Tia needs any encouragement."

Although Erika started working on the script that evening, she didn't tell Terri about that or what she would do tomorrow.

I want to avoid the ratchet trap, even with Terri, so only Chicky knows what's coming her way…

Erika took an early morning train to DC, arriving in time to treat Chicky to lunch while listening to her current track and field story.

"While you've been studying at that Manhattan Community College, I've been doing the same at George Washington U in DC, but even more; I made the varsity track team."

"That's the main reason I'm here. I have an assignment to write a script I can use when interviewing high school athletes who have a shot at an athletic scholarship. Can we role-play somewhere?"

"Sounds like a deal. Let's go back to my place."

Erika began the interview ninety minutes later.

"How would you compare male versus female athletic ability and motivation?"

"Other than in brute strength contests, the best females are closer to males than spectators realize. And it's a myth being disproved today that females don't like to compete. They do and show much more emotion than guys."

"How do you handle the stress of competition?"

"If I've got what it takes, I don't feel any stress or anxiety. I morph it into the thrill of racing, which is pretty much the same, win or lose."

"What about excuses if you don't win? What do you tell yourself?"

"I don't need any as long as I've tried my best. And even in sports like gymnastics and figure skating, where judges rather than stopwatches or tape measures tell us who won, the crowd and competitors will boo any gross violation."

"What's your view on discrimination holding back the best minority athletes?"

"That was the case long ago. Think about how long it took major league baseball to combine its stats with those of the Black Baseball League. We're much better today."

"And my last question is this: would you risk taking a drug that would guarantee a place on the podium but in ten years might cause a major medical issue?"

"Sure. For an athlete, ten years is like being in another century."

Erika leaned back after placing her script on the sofa and waited for Chicky to score her performance.

"Now, that's the way to interview an up-and-coming student-athlete. You get a gold medal."

"Thank you, thank you. I'd like to stay longer, but I have to get back. Next time we're together, let's hold a Cadre reunion by including X-O and Edward."

"That's a deal. I'll let-em know what to expect the next time you're in town."

CHAPTER 3

"A Star is Born"

AUGUST 2226

"Miss Tarrant, please report to my office."

"Yes, Ms. Casciato, I'm on my way." Even though she had no idea why she was being summoned to her boss's office, she hustled to find out. She knew she should never keep Tia waiting.

When entering a few minutes later, she guessed the reason when she spotted a film editor sitting next to a player connected to a monitor. The video started as soon as Terri seated herself in the only other chair.

Tia started talking ten minutes later.

"What comments would you like to make regarding its contents and editing?"

"Well, I tried to follow orders by preparing an interview script and, after watching the rough cut, finding some articles to support what I would say in the voiceover. I thought the editor did a masterful job getting to the final cut."

"He did, and so did you. I am slotting your high school athletes' story for this week. Congratulations. It will appear on the Times Website and run on local news."

Terri tried to maintain a seasoned journalist's composure.

"I'm pleased it meets your expectations. When might I expect a second assignment?"

"That's what I am about to describe..."

Terri floated through the rest of her workday, and the feeling carried her into the kitchen, where Erika focused on every word while the duo ate dinner.

"Thanks to your secret ghostwriting, Tia loves the video; it'll run on local news this week. And after she went over my next assignment, she said I'm a potential star in the making but warned me not to gloat. I won't, but could you give me some advice on how to behave?"

"Let me think about it; I'll tell you what I come up with when you tell me about your next assignment. Why don't you relax while I clean up here? We can talk later."

Erika knew who to talk with for advice on any topic, so she logged onto her workstation. Electra waited for Erika to explain what she needed.

"Terri's first video's a hit. Her boss says she's a potential star but warned her not to gloat. Terri asked me for some advice on handling herself at work, and you're my singular consultant, so what should I tell her?"

"Why not take the biblical route for proper attitudes and behaviors? Start by listing the Seven Deadly Sins from worst to least. Do you remember them?"

"I think I'd list them in this order—Pride, Greed, Lust, Envy, Gluttony, Wrath, and Sloth. Did I get it right?"

Electra's expression matched her pixyish tone.

"Yes, and I'm proud you did, but I'm using the word 'proud' to mean pleased or satisfied with someone, not boastful about yourself."

"OK, but what can she do to put a positive spin on it?"

"Tell her to pick and choose from the Seven Heavenly Virtues. I'll let you take it from here, but please notice that the number seven reappears often. Mere mortals can't keep track of more items than that. Now, please carry on."

Terri talked with the film crew the next day to learn the details of her next assignment. Then, after supper, she continued yesterday's discussion with Erika while they sat in the family room.

"I don't need an interview script, but I need to learn as much as possible about personal self-defense, especially for females. The crew will film a trainer teaching me the basics. I'm counting on you to write the voiceover and give me some training that'll make me look like a quick study."

"I assume the final cut will be about ten minutes. When will the cameras roll?"

"The last week of the month, so the pressure's off; you have two weeks to get me ready."

"Not a problem, and I can prep you right now for how to act. Do you remember the Seven Heavenly Virtues?"

"You've gotta be kidding. Hardly anyone can rattle them off. What are they?"

"Humility, Temperance plus Fortitude, Chastity, Justice, Faith, Hope, and Charity. The first four are the Cardinal Virtues, and the last three are Theological ones. And your boss's warning says you should show humility. You're smart, so use the others when you need to."

"If everyone did that all the time, maybe people wouldn't need self-defense training. But maybe they would. The 3-D world will always be dangerous until humans either evolve to something nicer or go extinct. Whatcha think about that?"

"I think we should always keep our self-defense skills sharp."

Erika had fun preparing for a voiceover, but even more when coaching Terri on some self-defense moves. She even taught some offensive ones Terri could use if the opportunity presented itself.

Terri looked and listened to everything when the crew leader introduced her to the self-defense trainer at his gym. He fit the look—a wiry-muscled early-thirties guy sporting a shaved head along with a meticulously groomed beard—and his words did the same.

"Relax. I'll do all the talking and explain what I'm going to demonstrate. They're some of the basic defensive moves I teach female students, and I'll talk you through them. And near the fifteen-minute mark, which'll be the end, I'll explain why females must be ready to go on offense. You can then try any of the moves I used. Any questions?"

"No, but your talking might eliminate any voiceover. The editor will make the call when we look at the video."

Everyone took their places; filming started as soon as the leader signaled. Terri followed every move the instructor called for, and he seemed pleased that Terri countered some of his. He picked up the pace as she blocked more of his attacks, and when he yelled, "Go on offense," she unleashed a move Erika had taught her.

Terri used a two-handed grab of his jersey to pull him close before diving backward onto the mat and thrusting one foot into his chest. The combined force generated by her foot and body pitched him over her head and into the camera equipment, scattering the crew and bringing an unexpected end to the session.

The crew clustered around the student and instructor, helping them up. Fifteen minutes later, when everything was back in order, the instructor gave his parting remarks.

"You pass, not with flying colors, but with an instructor flying over your head. Where'd you learn that move?"

"From a friend. I think it worked pretty well."

"It did, in fact, so well your video editor might want you to do a voiceover. But either way, I must congratulate our rising star."

"Thanks for the compliment, but I'm only one part of the show. You and the crew made me look that way today."

The crew chief had the last word.

"Starting tomorrow, Terri will help with the editing. Then we'll know how good she looks."

Terri's dinnertime description of today's filming kept Erika laughing, which stopped only when Terri finished.

"I'll write your voiceover script as soon as you and the editor finish the final cut, but you might not need my help on the next one if what you just said matches what I see."

"Don't say that; we're a team, remember? And as the boss keeps giving me more complicated assignments, I'll need it even more."

"Do you realize you're halfway through the time period Tia said she'd be your boss? And at the rate you're rolling, she might promote you even before the end of the year."

"I hope she doesn't. I'm feeling more and more comfortable right where I am."

"Let me remind you about our career discussion when you graduated. You never want to get too comfortable when starting out. You must keep pushing and challenging yourself. That's the only way you'll reach your full potential. If you stop pushing, you'll violate the Peter Principle."

"The what?"

"I came across it when surfing about jobs and careers. Management consultant Laurence Peter's principle holds in traditional hierarchical organizations and says employees get promoted based on their success in previous jobs until they reach a level at which they're no longer competent, and you're nowhere near it. Just stay humble and keep pushing ahead."

"How do you remember all this stuff?"

"I'm good at thinking, and if I forget some details, I surf to fill them in."

"OK, you keep thinking, and I'll keep doing. This combination might take us to unexpected places, but we'll handle whatever comes as we roll on…"

CHAPTER 4

"Rolling On"

OCTOBER 2226

Terri's rise to stardom rolled on. She won applause from film crews and editors alike for the quality of her videos while maintaining an unpretentious image at the office, and she deflected the advances of some senior reporters when they started hitting on her by fabricating a boyfriend supposedly pursuing a graduate degree
at Northwestern University's Medill School of Journalism. As she completed more assignments, she felt the pressure drop, thanks primarily to Erika's secret ghostwriting.

Erika occasionally felt a thump in her chest when Terri's assignments posed a challenge, but the more she handled them, the less of a problem the thumps became, and by the midpoint of the month, she felt comfortable enough to take a day off by visiting Chicky again.

She had to make a mad dash to catch the early morning train to Washington, DC. When she dropped into a seat after leaping aboard the last car, her thoughts registered excitement and concern.

Besides Chicky, I haven't visited my Cadre friends for almost a year… I don't know what they're up to… maybe she'll get us together… but she sounded concerned about something she wouldn't tell me over the phone…damn my heart's thumping so fast after running to catch the train…I sure hope my heart murmur won't cause a problem…

Having texted her when five minutes away from her apartment, Chicky greeted her at the front door.

"We can talk in private. Ma won't be home until 6 p.m."

"How about we order lunch? I'll pay when it gets here?"

"I should pay because I need your advice, but I need to save my dough so you can. Thanks."

Chicky settled Erika in a living room chair across from the sofa after placing the order, and they waited in awkward silence until Erika spoke.

"I sat on the sofa with you in the chair the last time I was here, and before I left, I asked if you'd set up a Cadre meeting the next time I visit. Do you want to do that?"

"I don't want a Cadre get-together until I know what I'm gonna do."

"So please tell me, what's the problem?"

Chicky glanced out the window briefly before refocusing while leaning toward Erika.

"I'm pregnant; you're the first person who knows, and I'm sure you can figure out who knocked me up."

Erika's thirty-second pause said Chicky's revelation had flummoxed her to the max.

"OK, let's think this through. I see two choices–the first is to get an abortion, and the second is to give birth–but that has three options; put the baby up for adoption, keep it and get married, or keep it and become a single mom. Have you—"

"I've already made the choice, and I'll tell you the reason I won't get an abortion. Ma waited until I graduated to tell me her story; I was born out of wedlock because she refused to get one and wanted me. She shamed Pa into marrying her, and all that got her was abuse and beatings."

"When do you plan to tell your mom?"

"Tonight, after you've gone back to Manhattan."

"What about X-O?"

"When my baby bump shows. Until then, I keep doing what I'm doing."

"What's X-O doing now?"

"He passed a car mechanic certification course and works at a buddy's garage."

Erika pulled back and thought for a minute before talking.

"OK, here's the deal. You must tell your GWU counselor about your condition. As long as you're in good academic standing with the university and don't voluntarily withdraw from the track team, it's against federal law to reduce your financial aid or scholarship in the event of pregnancy or childbirth."

Chicky held Erika's hands in hers before saying,

"I knew I could count on your advice."

"I'm not done. Take your mom to a government health counselor to find out what programs are right for you. And after you and your mom know what's coming, tell X-O before you tell anyone else."

Erika paused long enough to let the emotional stress subside, hoping that would stop her heart from thumping. And while doing that, she thought of something she and Chicky should do.

"Let's log on to your computer. There's a bunch of articles you should read."

Five minutes later, Erika said more.

"Many female track stars set records after having a baby. One of the best examples is the great Norwegian marathoner, Ingrid Kristiansen. She set a marathon world record not too long after giving birth. I've given you all the advice I have, so I'm saying goodbye, but why don't you read more articles until your mom gets home?"

"That's a deal. I'll call you after me and Ma have things lined up."

Chicky hugged Erika tight before letting go. She had to; Erika had promised to pay for the lunch order that had just arrived.

A satisfying lunch and celestine sky matched Erika's mood and made for a pleasant amble back to the subway, and it triggered her call while waiting on the platform. She spoke as soon as she recognized the voice.

"Hello, Edward, it's Erika. I'm in town and have a couple of hours before leaving. I'm about to catch the subway back to Union Station. Would you like to meet for a snack nearby if you're free?"

"Why yes. Shall I pick a place? We can be there in an hour."

"Please do…"

When Edward rose to greet her, Erika felt their friendship come to the fore.

"You look even smarter than before. College must be to your liking. Please tell me what you're doing?"

Ten minutes later, Erika knew his polite personality was even better than before.

"So, you've got a full scholarship at GWU, and you're majoring in political science."

"And what about you? Are you going to college in Manhattan?"

"I'm taking courses at Manhattan Community College while working part time. I found an intern position doing background research on topics that New York Times journalists are working on."

"Your surfing skill should make that easy."

"But the harder part is analyzing what I find. Deadlines are challenging, and some topics take me where I haven't been before."

"That's a great place for a poli-sci major. Too bad I'm not an intern there with you. It'd be like our high school community projects, but on steroids."

"Hey, you've just triggered an idea. I can pay when I need your help. You can work remotely and send me your analysis. And we'll keep this a secret. Whatcha think?"

"This has possibilities; tell me more."

By the time Erika caught her train, Edward was on board with their secret spy mission.

Terri breezed through the next assignment that earned her an even better one, which the crew scheduled for early November. Terri gave the topic to Erika, who said she'd have Terri's voiceover and training ready to roll by then, and the topic resonated with Edward when she relayed it to him.

"Gun violence and military weapons training are correlated, and online videos plus illegal gun purchases put too many high-powered guns in the hands of thugs. Hunters don't need automatic weapons."

"I agree. Make that the focus of your analysis. I'll do the rest…"

Terri's crew prepped her for the shoot. A gun range instructor would show her how to use an automatic and then let her run through an attack simulation on an obstacle course. He started talking when the crew chief said, "Go."

"Today, I'll show reporter Terri Tarrant how to use the M4A1 carbine. It's the primary weapon used by Navy SEAL teams. It's a shorter, more compact version of the M16A2 rifle, which is specially designed for U.S. Special Operations Forces. Terri, are you ready?"

Terri's tone matched her SEAL uniform.

"I'm good to go."

And she was better than good. She mastered locking, loading, and slamming in magazine reloads as fast as new recruits, and she navigated the obstacle course like a seasoned veteran.

The instructor talked to the crew as they were about to leave.

"Terri made your job easy. You needed only a couple of retakes."

Then he pointed a question at her.

"Where'd you develop your athleticism?"

"I led my high school cheerleading team."

"Well, it certainly gave you all the right moves."

"Thank you for the compliment, but the camera crew called the shots. I simply pulled the trigger."

"And what a deadly pull you have. I know some journalists travel to war zones, and I hope you never need to use it if you move into those kinds of assignments."

"I don't control my assignments, but if I get one that puts me in danger, my crew will know what to do."

CHAPTER 5

"Moving Up"

DECEMBER 2226

"Miss Tarrant, please report to my office."

"Yes, Ms. Casciato, I'm on my way." Unlike the summons from several months ago, Terri could guess what she might hear. Tia waited for Terri to close the door and seat herself before speaking.

"I told you six months ago you would be either promoted or fired by the end of the year. I am pleased to report that you have earned the former, not the latter. During this time period, you have distinguished yourself by thoroughly researching your assigned topics and scripting your voiceovers. Congratulations are in order."

But Terri would not have guessed what happened next. Tia's last sentence cued the following procession: a video editor strode in, followed by a camera crew pushing a cart loaded with a celebration cake and assorted beverages, and a gaggle of newsroom people right behind. Tia came to Terri but waited for the commotion to settle down before continuing.

"You are now one of our special projects staff reporters assigned to the socio-political beat, which will include both domestic and international assignments. You will continue working out of this location, but starting January 1st you will report to one of our senior syndicated anchors. And we expect your skill to level up to even higher standards."

Terri's quick wits helped her figure out what to say after shaking Tia's hand and turning to the people gathered around her.

"This celebration is for the editors and crew as well as for me. They're the ones who made me look good in the final cuts. And I hope I can do half as good a job cutting the cake."

Although the rest of Terri's workday became a blur as she started preparing to move up, she had the big picture in focus when she shared the news at dinner with Erika.

"My H.R. counselor gave me some guidelines for what to do until I formally meet my new boss, which happens right after New Years. Maybe you can start thinking about the important domestic and international socio-political issues. That'll reduce the risk of being blindsided by an upcoming assignment. And the pressure's off for the rest of the year. It's like we're starting the Holiday Season early."

"This will make for an even better quarter break at school. And don't fret, I'll think about how to handle the political beat."

While Terri kept chatting about the day, Erika made a comment to herself.

I know someone even better than Edward to help, but I won't contact them until Terri meets the new boss. I can relax until then...

"Mother and Father invited us to spend the Holidays with them. If you're up for it, I'll drive us this Saturday evening. It'll be a relaxing change of pace from working all day on job change activities at the office."

"Please count me in."

The girls had packed the car before Terri drove to the office, so Erika waited in the cold air outside their apartment in the glimmering darkness that heightened all her senses. She shared private thoughts meant only for herself, triggered when flashing headlights signaled Terri approaching.

I feel a breathless joy when I'm with her...it pulls me into an emotional state I hope will never leave...like the thrill of driving in a convertible with the top down and the wind whipping through my hair...but I can't tell her...it might break the spell...does she feel the same?... I'm afraid to ask...just leave it be...

Terri hugged her before driving away, then glanced her way again.

"What's wrong? Your cheeks are streaked with tears."

"The cold air did it. I'm OK now."

"Good; I am too; the same will apply to Mother and Father when we tell them what we've been doing. Isn't it nice we have an entire week to tell them?"

"I agree."

Mrs. Tarrant hugged both girls simultaneously while Mr. Tarrant watched from close by before toting their luggage to Terri's adolescent bedroom. The girls took only minutes to freshen up before coming to the kitchen, and fifteen minutes later, Mr. Tarrant carved the roast beef at the dining room table while serving his guests first. Mrs.Tarrant pointed most questions at Terri, which gave Erika enough time to comment while observing.

Terri's lucky to have actual parents, giving her memories she'll have forever. I don't, but I have Electra…

Terri gave answers her parents liked until one stumped her.

"A school reunion? I never go to them. I'm too young. It's too soon to get together with classmates who haven't done much yet and talk about the good old days. Ask Erika what she thinks."

Erika waited for Mrs. Tarrant to do so before answering.

"I agree with Terri, but I would add that my closest friends are like family, and I'd want to see them several times a year, which I do when visiting DC."

"How nice. Will you do that this time?"

"No, I'd rather spend it with Terri and you folks."

The week proved so relaxing that Terri decided they'd spend the week before New Years back in Manhattan. Erika suggested they call Ava to wish them a Happy New Year, and when they did, Ava said even more.

"Why not spend New Year's Eve with Ivana and me? We'll take you club dancing."

"Wonderful. What time should we come to your place, and what should we wear?"

"Get here by seven, and wear whatever you feel like dancing the night away in."

"OK, see you then."

Everything lined up for Ava to whisk them to a club catering to all preferences, and its ambiance impressed Erika.

"I love the mini-lights that synch with the music. And everyone's so comfortable with all the sex pairings."

Terri added more.

"The males have better dance moves than the females, even when the female leads. And I thought my cheerleading moves would get looks."

Ivana filled in when Terri paused.

"You do look good in sexy dress. Come, dance with me. Ava, go dance with Erika."

And so they did until the crowd counted down to cheer "Happy New Year" before singing Auld Lange Syne. As the foursome shared kisses, Erika knew more but said it only to herself.

The song may be about times long past, but what I'm feeling right now will always be a part of me, and so will the excitement I feel about the future.

The girls puttered about the apartment all weekend, ensuring Terri would be ready to meet her new boss first thing Monday morning. And she was. Terri reported the highlights at supper that evening.

"Mrs. Walthers is a ball-buster, just like Tia, but she coats it with a thicker layer of civility, which is good for a syndicated anchor. But she did stress I must be even better at researching and scripting."

Erika felt a momentary heart thump, then asked,

"Did she mention what your first assignment might be?"

"No itinerary or deadline yet, but I'll travel to major metropolitan areas, interviewing leading universities and corporations for their take on recent graduates before talking with a sample of students and newer employees. How does that sound?"

"Like I better start prepping on my own while you do yours at the office. But don't worry, I'll be ready when you are."

Erika calmed herself while riding the early morning train to Washington to meet Edward and Monet at her embassy office.

I'm doing fine. I've prioritized everything for my schoolwork and ghost writing by checking how much effort and time are required. Monet and Edward must have done the same. How nice they fit me in…

After her usual diplomatic segue, Monet let Erika start the discussion.

"I'm now reporting to a syndicated anchor. It's a step up but will demand better and faster work. The first assignment will involve traveling to interview leaders at top universities and businesses in major cities about recent grads and new employees and then talking to a sample of young people. What issues do you think will come up?"

Monet nodded for Edward to start.

"Here's what college counselors and students would say. Schools are too expensive; there are few jobs after graduation that lead to a meaningful career, which means young people are emphasizing health and happiness in their personal lives over slaving away at work."

Monet continued when Edward's shrug said he had finished.

"We can extend that to what employers say. Washington's economic policies continue economic polarization between the elites and everyone else. And this skews capitalism's investment toward infrastructure rather than labor.

"Furthermore, historical evidence on a global scale shows that the trends continue upsetting the balance between humanity and civilization, which we see in the clash between China and the United States, the impact of artificial intelligence, and the viral threats posed by new life forms. We have listed too much to assimilate today, so let's prioritize for Erika…"

Erika's confidence increased with every mile traveled on the way back to New York.

I have everything under control, and I'll tell Terri when I get home. I'll be happy to see her, and she'll be happy to hear the news.

CHAPTER 6

"The Road Warriors"

FEBRUARY 2227

Terri's imaginative storytelling rivaled Erika's but with one difference: Terri delighted in sharing hers, but Erika was afraid to tell hers to anyone but herself. Nevertheless, she always loved hearing Terri's, the latest of which she spun after getting her first assignment from her new boss, Mrs. Walthers.

"We're going to be a team of Road Warriors, traveling to record interviews I'll help edit into a montage, just like a movie producer does with scenes to segue to the message they want to get across."

"When do we start?"

"Late February. We'll interview big-name universities, businesses, and recent graduates or new employees to uncover their concerns, and we'll travel to major cities as soon as Mrs. Walthers tells her contacts to get ready. They'll have a crew and contacts lined up. All I have to do is book our flights and tell them when we'll arrive at their offices."

Terri paused for the plural pronoun to register.

"You mean I'm coming along?"

"Sure; I'll simply tell everyone who asks that you're my assistant, helping with logistics and travel arrangements. After that, no one's going to look any further. My assertive personality will get us where we want to go, and your clever words will smooth over any rough edges I might leave in our wake."

Erika's expression told Terri she liked what she was hearing.

"This'll keep me from getting bored, and I'll have no trouble handling my online class assignments."

"And remember, we travel light. Pack only one set of leisure and two sets of professional clothes. I'll buy whatever else we need and pick up the meal tabs. Isn't that a nice journalist job perk?"

"Let me add one more. We don't have to make the beds or clean up any messes. And we should pack a pair of exercise shoes. Just check the fitness centers before you book us into the hotels."

Terri's team worked their plan to perfection on the first trip. They warmed up in New York before traveling to Chicago. Erika's New York experiences researching and scripting made interviews and filming a breeze, and she found the iconic Lou Malnatti's deep-dish pizza, which the team liked as much as New York style. Ditto for Houston and its tacos al carbon at Ninfas Tex Mex chain, followed by an LA diner whose servers look like Hollywood stars. And finally, to San Francisco's Bubba Gump Shrimp Company Restaurant on Pier 39, which is a short walk to Fisherman's Wharf.

Erika forced Terri to join her every morning in the fitness center, which energized them for the day ahead and burned enough calories to keep ahead of the fun-filled dinners. Meanwhile, Terri used Erika to shield her from journalists hitting on her too often.

Upon returning to home base, Erika concentrated on school while Terri edited all the way to the final cut, which a senior editor approved by the end of March. Terri knew the video would be a winner but didn't advertise it. She waited for Mrs. Walthers to summon her, which she did the third week of April. Terri knew the drill by now and sat primly in front of the desk.

"Since you seem to sharpen your skills on every assignment, I shall give you an even more challenging one. I am moving you up to the political beat. Your next assignment is to assess the political ramifications of your previous one, and this time, you will not crisscross the country. You will start in Washington by interviewing selected members of Congress and the heads of national agencies. Then, you will compare what you find there with what the presidents of Ivy League universities and some of the consulting companies they spawned have to say."

"When will you give me my contact list and deadline?"

Mrs. Walthers slid a packet of stapled papers across the desk before answering.

"I like your attitude. You'll find everything you need here. I think you'll find the end of May acceptable."

"Thank you for your confidence; I shall make it so."

Terri's enthusiasm positively bubbled into her summary when talking with Erika that evening.

"We're moving into what people really want to listen to on the news. We're getting a chance to connect topics of interest to what leading politicians and government agencies in DC are saying. I follow that up by interviewing top Ivy League universities to find out what they're doing. All you have to do for the next assignment is link them to what we covered in the last one. Think you'll be ready by the end of May?"

Erika felt a heart thump that subsided before she replied.

"You know, I'm settling into the groove. I can balance it against online exam preparations, so please don't worry. And think about this—you can indirectly use your last name and Columbia credentials to get special treatment."

"I hadn't thought about that. We'll see if it works."

The team's implementation of this assignment unfolded even more smoothly than the previous ones. Halfway through, when Terri said, "Practice makes perfect," Erika looked ready to put a different spin on the trope.

"No, it's 'Perfect practice makes perfect.' The role-playing we did made your questions flow so naturally that even the most devious politicos couldn't fake an answer, nor could the agency administrators hide the Administration's actual intentions."

"And some of them said my Father should be proud of my career. How about that?"

"Don't forget to include your Mother."

"I won't. You think we'll have as much success interviewing the universities?"

"Why not? Just strike a thoughtful, philosophical tone and mention that you learned it at Columbia. And how nice we're starting in Boston. After that, the rest will be easier. Just build on what you do there."

Erika's prediction came true. By the end of June, Terri had her next assignment, the details of which she shared early that evening.

"Mrs. Walthers says the viewers like my fresh face and enthusiasm; they say I give clear explanations, and that's why our next assignment takes us to the intersection of DOD and government labs with Silicon Valley and weapons development. There's a lot of science and technology in it, and you'll have to summarize it for me and the viewers. Think you can handle that?"

Erika's heart kept thumping when she answered.

"Where will we go? And what's the deadline?"

"We'll start at the Pentagon, then go to Los Alamos, and end up in Silicon Valley. I already have my contact list, so we can start once you've got my script. We've got until the end of August to make the final cut, so it's doable, isn't it?"

"Lemme think about it."

Erika went to her workstation, hiding the rising panic from Terri, but she knew she needed help that only one entity could supply. Electra's avatar appeared moments later, waiting for Erika to unload her woe, and when Erika had nothing else to say, Electra looked happy to reply.

"Leave all the math and science to me. I've dealt with even harder issues several lifetimes ago. I'll brief you before your road trip begins and summarize what your contacts say. Then, all you have to do is wordsmith to satisfy Terri and the editors. We'll be good if you keep your laptop turned on so I can spy from the Cyberspace shadows. Now, please calm down."

Reading relief flooding through Erika's expression, Electra's avatar left the screen.

Terri's mastery of basic science and technology impressed film crews and subject matter experts. She astutely segued from one interviewee to the next and connected the locations. And when ending the final cut, she added her personal thoughts.

"Modern technology today gives weapons that let mankind obliterate itself, and all that previous civilizations we have created. I think we might gain a better appreciation of what's in store if we humans don't heed our better angels by reading 'Nuclear War–a Scenario' by Pulitzer Prize-winner Annie Jacobsen.

"It graphically tells what would happen in a nuclear exchange between superpowers–in the first twenty-four minutes, then the next twenty and twenty-four more, then the next twenty-four months and beyond, which is a grim outcome if governments are foolish enough to ignore the consequences.

"This is New York Times reporter Terri Tarrant signing off."

Mrs. Walthers loved it all.

CHAPTER 7

"Sex Comes Knocking"

OCTOBER 2227

Terri and Erika settled so comfortably and inconspicuously into their technique for handling Terri's assignment lineup that no one at her office noticed anything other than the quality of her work and humility whenever receiving praise.

Erika told none of her classmates about her extracurricular assignments, which meant she blended in like a normal college junior, except for one characteristic that had been building for the past year: her fascination with college guys. When it reached the point of near obsession, she knew she needed to talk with someone, so she took the mid-October Saturday early morning train to Washington, thinking all the way.

Chicky told me a couple of years ago her hormones were ahead of mine. She's still ahead… after all, she's been a single mom for a year…but I'm catching up. I need her advice…

Chicky and her mom greeted her at the front door. Erika hugged Chicky after admiring the one-year-old being held by Chicky's mom, and Chicky took her to the living room for a one-on-one talk, which Erika started.

"Your daughter looks happy, as does your mom, but you look tired. Does X-O help much?"

"He gives me money when he can, but he stopped taking more mechanic cert courses once Zena was born. He says he can't pay me while paying for courses."

"Are you still taking classes at GWU?"

"No, and as you can see, I don't have time for running track, but thanks to Ma, I'm taking courses at U of DC Community College and working part time at the bookstore. That's me, but what about you? What's on your mind?"

Erika shifted uncomfortably for a moment before locking eyes.

"Sex; I can't stop thinking about guys I see at school."

"Anyone in particular/"

"No. Sometimes, all I want is to ride around in their cars with my skirt up and the windows down while screaming. Was it like that for you?"

"Now you know what all the fuss is about. But you gotta be careful. Don't let it get outta control. You don't wanna get knocked up for no good reason."

"What about now? Do you still want to have sex?"

"Not many nice guys wanna date single moms, so I don't get many offers, but that's OK. My sex drive's still there, but it's less than before."

Having heard enough, Erika shifted to a tamer topic.

"Thanks for sharing; we've talked enough about sex, so why don't you and your mom show me what it's like taking care of Zena?"

"That's a deal. Let's do it…"

Chicky's advice helped. Erika's focus on male classmates subsided, but not enough to keep her from initiating foreplay at a Halloween Party. Only masks and another couple stumbling into the bedroom protected her identity.

Contacting Electra the next evening, Erika spoke first.

"I've got a problem; I'm thinking too much about sex. I'm embarrassed to tell Terri, but I talked to a high school friend because we talked about sex way back then."

Electra's expression matched her understanding tone.

"Please tell me what Chicky told you and what's happening now."

Electra spoke again fifteen minutes later.

"Sex is part of being human, just like eating and sleeping. It's always there and always will be until your hormones give out, which for you won't happen for a long time. So, don't feel embarrassed; simply adjust your attitude."

"What about telling Terri?"

"Do that when the time is right."

"But how will I know?"

"You'll know, just like you'll know when you find someone with all the right chemistry. It'll be like a lightning bolt or an emotional chain reaction."

"So, what should I do now?"

"You want to keep sampling so you know what sex is like. Just keep it from hijacking your rational self into the danger zone. That will keep you safe."

Electra's avatar vanished in the wink of her eye.

CHAPTER 8

"A Break to Remember"

DECEMBER 2227

Both Road Warriors had all serious issues under control when Terri flipped the calendar to the last month of the year and explained what they needed to do.

"Mrs. Walthers hasn't given me the details yet but says I'd better prepare for our first international assignment, which will have more risk than domestic ones, but should keep us out of danger zones. I'll start preparing by talking with some Times foreign correspondents and then with Washington contacts who've become friends. What about you?"

"I'll set up some meetings, but I hope I know the details before I visit some of mine. Until then, I'll prep for final exams with some classmates. Let me know when you've got the details."

"Did you pick smart ones? I'll let you know as soon as I get them. After that, we can decide what we'll do until we leave."

"Good. I hope we can take a break to remember friends and family."

"Me too."

Erika preferred not to mention that her smart classmate meetings would be one-on-one with only guys; from her point of view, she had sex under control.

There's no harm in flirting. Guys like the peek they get while I toy with them by writing some of their essays and promising them more if they meet my standards that I change to fit my mood, which they can never guess.

Erika kept balancing toying and studying until Terri told her the details of the upcoming assignment.

"We'll leave early in January to interview young people in war-threatened Latvia, which is waging a mini-proxy battle between

Russia and Western Europe. If we can finish our preparation meetings before Christmas, we can visit my parents."

"I'll schedule mine for tomorrow and will let you know when I'm set for our trip."

"And I'll set up more for me in DC when I finish what I've got going at the office. Good luck to both of us."

Monet spoke first when she greeted Erika at her Embassy office

"Edward should speak first. He has the best point of view on how war damages youth."

Edward spoke in his typical measured tone.

"We hate the invaders for robbing us of our present and future, and we hate our politicians for not taking action earlier to protect us, but most of us won't defend the homeland unless allies give us weapons and training. Without them, it's a lost cause. That's the universal cry."

Monet added, "And it becomes more complex in Europe; the Balkan states share ethnic minorities that often want to break away, and Russia considers the Baltic states a defensive buffer against the West. Unfortunately, Russia has taken an offensive posture for which France, Germany, and Austria still quarrel over containing an enemy that provides energy resources.

"But you can stay out of harm's way if you avoid visiting cities that are too close to the border. Zoom or Skype interviews will work almost as well, as will the videos that show population and infrastructure collateral damage."

"Would you two give me a list of questions to ask students and government officials?"

"We'll do that until you feel you have enough..."

Terri looked pleased the next evening when she looked at the list.

"Wow, all you have to do is wordsmith them into a script. That settles it; we'll drive to my parents a few days before Christmas and return when we've had enough of a break."

Terri's good intentions couldn't carry past Christmas Eve. Mrs. Tarrant became ill the next morning and insisted the girls spend the days between now and the upcoming trip in Manhattan.

Erika told Terri the next day to call Ava.

"We had fun last New Year's Eve with Ava and Ivana at a dance club. Why not have a repeat?"

"Let's find out what they say."

They liked the idea, and this year they would go to a new club. Ava gave them the address, and after the call, Erika found its Website.

"It looks nice and safe; close enough too; we can take the subway."

Erika didn't mention that dancing with young guys would be even better than chatting, but she couldn't hide her enthusiasm once the foursome settled at a table. She caught the eye of a guy who took her to the dance floor fifteen minutes later and stayed at it for nearly ninety more.

Ava cautioned her when she came back for a drink.

"We don't know any of the people. That's why the rest of us are watching instead of dancing, so be careful who you dance with."

"I will. There are lots of good-looking guys to choose from."

When one of them came and took her away again, the remaining threesome continued conversing about the past and coming year, but Ivana did more Erika-watching than talking.

An hour later, Ivana strode alone onto the dance floor. The number of couples built as midnight approached, but she had more on her mind than wishing Happy New Year. When reaching a flushed-looking Erika, she tore her from the clutches of her older and sweaty partner before yelling.

"You no good for my friend. Leave us."

"What the?... I oughta slug both of—" Ivana's quick kick between the legs put him on the floor. Ivana pulled Erika back to the table as a sea of dancers' legs swallowed him.

Ivana had to speak. Neither Ava nor Terri had seen the confrontation, and Erika was still too stunned.

"Erika too man-hungry. I pull her away this time, but she better calm down before something really bad happen."

No one spoke until Terri did, after glancing around the table.

"Thank you for keeping her safe tonight. It's too late now, so let's go home, but I'll tell her tomorrow. I'm sure this break has been one for her to remember."

CHAPTER 9

"Into the Danger Zones"

JANUARY 2228

Erika tried her best to look penitent for most of the New Year's Day morning lecture Terri gave, and her voice sounded that way when she finally had a chance to talk.

"I learned last night that it's dangerous teasing guys I don't know very well. Their points of view differ from mine, and I don't want to cross into their danger zones."

"Don't stop there. What about guys you do know pretty well?"

"I guess I shouldn't tease them, either. It makes me look like I'm too full of myself."

"That's why you should start practicing humility. You're the one who reminded me over a year ago about the Seven Deadly Sins and Virtues. And you should pay attention to other danger zones."

"Which ones?"

"Look, I know you're smart, but you have to pay more attention to your surroundings. The adult world is dangerous. Just walking on a new street or entering a new place can be risky. And where we're going for our first European assignment is extra risky. Do you remember where we're going and how we'll get around?"

"You said we'll fly to London and use Eurail to get to all the cities where the Times London office has set up our contacts. But why do we leave so late at night?"

"Come on, start thinking. To compensate for the time zone difference. London is five hours ahead of New York. We should be tired and have no trouble sleeping on the plane by leaving late. Then we wake fresh and ready to start the day on London time, feeling less jet-lagged."

Terri waited for Erika to comment, but she didn't, so Terri said more.

"I've got a special assignment for you. Start researching the difference in attitudes between Europeans and Americans, comparing young and old. While you're doing that, I'll take care of tickets, papers, and logistics. We're leaving next week on Friday evening, which gives us two weeks to get them done, so we each have our marching orders until then. OK?"

Erika looked like she agreed when she said,

"I promise to start thinking more."

Erika enjoyed working on this assignment more than on those for school, and the longer she worked, the more she liked it, especially the summary sheet she had just printed.

No matter the topic, this will make a useful framework when tabulating the information for each country subdivided into Young and Old. I don't need to do a statistical analysis; a qualitative, subjective analysis, from my point of view, will satisfy Terri's video viewers.

Terri doesn't need to see this, but I'll use it to construct her interview script for her first assignment and then write her voiceover for the final cut.

Hooray… time to take a break… I've got an entire week to surf for more information on our first assignment's topic…

Summary Sheet for Europe

Europe is a collection of Countries grouped into overlapping Organizations:
  - **NATO (North American Treaty Organization) for Security**
  - **EU (European Union) for Monetary and Economic Consolidation**

Geographic Groupings:
  - **Balkans**
  - **Baltics**
  - **Scandinavia**

Countries of Special Importance:
  - **Russia**
  - **England**

- **Germany**
- **France**

How to Characterize a Country's Personality:
- **Religion**
- **Philosophy**
- **Socio-Political Characteristics: Type of Government Attitudes Toward: Liberty Equality Capitalism Progress Integration Technology Climate Change**

Cultural Characteristics: Institutions Arts
Comparisons to Make:
- **Between Each Country and the United States**
- **Among Each Country**
- **Young to Old Within the Country and to the United States**

Noticing Terri's focus on trip preparation, Erika kept to herself until departure day before asking about packing.

"Pack two suitcases this morning holding your necessities. I'll do the same and get them picked up at noon for delivery to JFK. The weather's good, so we'll take the subway tonight. It connects to Airtrain, which is the best way to get to the airport. And remember to carry only your purse where you'll keep your cell phone, tickets, and I.D.s."

"What time's our flight?"

"It's British Airways leaving at 11:15 p.m. You can do the math to calculate arrival time. London is five hours ahead of New York, and the flight takes seven hours. We'll have a light dinner here and hike to the subway at eight. We can relax once the courier picks up our luggage. Remember to give them your laptop, too."

The excitement of her first international trip kept Erika from relaxing as much as she would have liked, but she kept it under control. The walk to the subway and the train ride gave her things to focus on, but unfortunately, one of them was her bladder.

She poked Terri as the train approached a station midway to JFK.

"I'm sorry, but I can't hold it. I have to pee."

"OK, we'll get off and find someplace with a restroom."

Leading them through a rundown neighborhood, Terri took them to a twenty-four-hour liquor store. When the clerk pointed where to go, Erika handed her purse to Terri and hustled away. Terri browsed the nearby aisle, hefting a bottle or two.

But when too many minutes elapsed, Terri knew she had better find out why. She didn't knock; she pushed into the restroom, and what she saw froze her.

Erika was kneeling in front of a man with his pants half-down while another pushed a gun to her head while shoving her head forward. Terri screamed, and her survival instincts took over when she bolted. She grabbed a bottle from the shelf and smashed it over the head of the guy still holding the gun, toppling him backward; Terri picked up the gun and charged into the bathroom. The guy still had his pants down and was punching Erika, but not for long.

Bang-bang. Terri fired two bullets that jerked him off. Terri hauled Erika to her feet and shoved one purse into her hands before hissing,

"Follow me."

Terri put the gun in her purse before racing out the rear door with Erika right behind.

Terri didn't speak again until they were on a deserted subway platform.

"Are you hurt?"

"No, but what are we going to do?"

"What do you suggest?"

"Shouldn't we go to the police?"

"And tell them what? In a perfect world, sure, but the world's not perfect. Look, no one knows who we are. I'll wipe any prints off the gun before I throw it where no one will find it, and then we'll board our flight. We tell no one what happened."

Erika didn't have time to say anything. Their train arrived, and Terri pushed her onboard. And as it pulled away, Erika had only one thought.

My heart's still pounding, but I'm beginning to settle down… thank god and Terri…we're both OK…we're leaving the scene of one danger zone, but we're heading to another…after tonight, I know I must always pay attention…

CHAPTER 10

"Dodging Bullets and Beyond"

JANUARY 2228

The girls pretended that nothing unusual had happened while traveling to London. Since this would be the first time anyone in the London office met them, Terri's coordinator, Fraser Nelson, a seasoned Times-BBC reporter, saw her as an enthusiastic young journalist worried about her first international assignment. He also liked the exterior, and after she introduced her assistant, Fraser gave her special treatment by explaining what to expect when covering the European beat.

"Well, my dear, now I see why Mrs. Walthers promoted you. An attractively packaged, youthful point of view will charm viewers of all persuasions."

"Thank you for the compliment, but she told me to be more than just a pretty face. That's why I want to get close to the action when interviewing people to experience what they are. Isn't that what you do?"

"Dodging bullets thrilled me in my younger days, but I don't move as fast now, so I am cautious. You're too young to heed my advice; all I will say is for you be to be watchful. And now, to the particulars of your first assignment. Please tell me what you know about the political climate in Latvia?"

Terri held her own, thanks to Erika's research, and Fraser heard enough to conclude the meeting a half-hour later.

"You will rendezvous with your crew in Riga, the capital, and proceed from there. Please tell me all about your adventures when you return."

"I will, and thank you for the briefing."

Erika enjoyed their travel on Eurail trains and buses to Riga after a two-hour shuttle flight took them to Berlin. The 750-mile ride gave her two days to alternate between surfing for information and viewing the landscapes of Poland and Latvia. Latvia's forests, wetlands, and rivers told her the country has a temperate climate, and her surfing said Riga is a European cultural center built on centuries of the Baltic states (Estonia, Latvia, and Lithuania) interconnected heritage, but Poland struck her differently.

The countryside looks homey, romantic, and desolate all at the same time. Some articles say the 20th and early 21st century wars destroyed much of Central and Eastern Europe. Nature reclaimed some of it, but Climate Change has reshaped it, too…

Terri listened to more of Erika's Latvian details.

"Half the two-million population lives in Riga, which is on the western side near the Baltic Sea. The next largest city is Daugavpils, which has a little over a hundred thousand and is near the Russian border.

"And get this–Latvia has the highest female-to-male population in Europe. Not only that, but Latvian women are the tallest in Europe and dominate the modeling world. We'll have to ask Ivana about this when we get back."

Not to be outdone, Terri fired back.

"Well, while you've been surfing and sightseeing, I've told the crew what I'd like, and here's what they've set up. We'll have a town hall meeting in Riga where I can use the script and questions you gave me. And a day later, they'll take us to a similar setup in Daugavpils, so we're copacetic. Let's take a break until we meet the crew."

The meeting took place early the next evening in a government building auditorium, which was more than large enough to hold the fifty people on the contact list. After reciting from Erika's memorized script, Terri made a standard remark.

"Now, before I ask my questions, would anyone like to make a comment?"

Only one older gentleman did.

"I commend you for doing your homework. You understand more about our country than most reporters who come here. I would just add that our flag, which is crimson red with a white horizontal stripe across, shows my country's willingness to fight for freedom. I think young and old share it, though they may have different ways of doing so."

After he sat, Terri continued.

"Thank you for adding that to what I know about your homeland. And now, to my questions…"

After the meeting ended, Erika stayed in the background, letting audience members congratulate her partner while the crew packed up to take them back to the hotel. Once in the room, Erika offered her thoughts.

"You positively nailed the interview. If you do the same day after tomorrow, editing for the final cut will be a breeze."

"Thanks for letting me know. I can't judge myself. That's why I rely on you."

"And that's why we make a great team. Now, take a warm shower to help cycle down."

Erika's prognosis proved true. The people in the audience and those who lived close to the border appreciated her concern for the country and her praise of their collective resolve to repel Russian incursions. And though no shells sailed overhead, she saw firsthand the damage done to homes and lives.

Soon after, the crew took Terri and Erika to a chopper port that flew them to Riga, where they caught a flight back to London. They went directly from the airport to the Times office, where Fraser greeted them.

"Goodness, aren't you the energetic ones. Are you ready to dive into video editing? Shall I take you to our senior editor this minute, or would you prefer some lunch?"

"Why not order something we can eat while working?"

"Very well, I shall order fish and chips for you, the editor, and your assistant. And I recommend a fizzy soda to complement what we Brits call our thoroughly greasy, delectable, magical meal."

Terri accepted his offer; Erika stayed in the background, enjoying lunch while observing the editor teach Terri even more.

Terri knew when the editor gave the final cut his stamp of approval and sent it to Mrs. Walthers that she would like it but not how much, so she tried to calm herself before answering the call coming from the Manhattan home office three days later.

Mrs. Walther's optimistic tone bolstered Terri's.

"You are sliding down the learning curve faster, and it's taking you beyond my expectations. Congratulations."

"That's high praise. I hope to continue earning it."

"You will, depending upon how well you handle the promotion. You are now our special projects reporter at large, working out of the London office and reporting to me. Fraser Nelson will coordinate your crews and contacts. The Times will pay for your short-term rental costs and will give you a satisfactory monthly meal allowance. Fraser will arrange for an apartment."

"What must I do?"

"Prepare at least one ten-to-thirty-minute video a month on a European topic of your choosing."

"Uh, how do I find them?"

"You seem more clever than most reporters; use your imagination to come up with some and then compare American to European views like you've been doing with your scripts and questions."

"And when will this start?"

"Officially, February 1st; use the time from now until that date to adjust to London and your new title. I have already informed Fraser, and I think you have everything you need from me, so please proceed."

When Terri talked to Fraser immediately after the call, he promised to find an apartment suitable for her and her assistant, then told her to go home and relax until tomorrow.

She took his advice and shared the news with Erika when she reached the hotel.

She wrapped up by saying,

"I'm so wound up I can barely see straight. What can I do to calm down?"

"We can meditate by walking on nearby streets, and we can—"

Terri slapped her forehead one time before interrupting.

"Jeez Louise, I'm sorry. Will staying with me be OK? I'll need your help more than ever developing topics, scripts and question lists."

"Sure. Remember, we're more than partners."

"I'm sorry I interrupted. What were you going to say?"

"Take a walk right now."

Terry was happy to let Erika lead the way.

CHAPTER 11

"Getting to Denmark"

FEBRUARY 2228

Erika knew how to proceed when Terri asked what "Getting to Denmark" meant.

"The phrase is a socio-political term that originated over a hundred years ago and became widely publicized in three books written by historian Francis Fukuyama–*Political Order and Political Decay, The Origins of Political Order,* and *The end of History and the Last Man.* He conjectures that all societies will become a capitalistic liberal democracy, but socio-political events in the last 150 years show the contrary. Glance through this handout and let me know when I should continue."

Erika gave her the handout and waited.

Facts About Denmark

- **The Danes, originally from Germany, settled in Denmark. The name means "Danes on the March," and they built a farming, fishing, and seafaring culture with its own language (Danish).**

- **Denmark, Sweden, Norway, and Finland comprise Scandinavia. Copenhagen, the capital, is on the eastern edge across from Sweden.**

- **Denmark is surrounded by water and controls Greenland. Denmark is approximately twice the size of Massachusetts.**

- **Denmark's population is six million. Seven-hundred-thousand live in Copenhagen. Capital's population density is 18,000 per square mile (two-thirds that of New York City). Denmark's density is 361 per square mile.**

- **Denmark is noted for good political and economic institutions. It is stable, democratic, peaceful, prosperous, inclusive, and has extremely low levels of political corruption.**
- **The politics of Denmark takes place within the framework of a parliamentary representative democracy, a constitutional monarchy, and a decentralized unitary state in which the monarch of Denmark is the head of state.**

What does "Getting to Denmark Mean?

- **Denmark might be a better model that developing countries can use to join the post-modern world.**
- **Better means than the United States or China.**
- **72% of Denmark's population belongs to the Evangelical Lutheran Church, but less than a fifth consider themselves "very religious."**
- **Martin Luther (1483–1546), a German monk and university professor, started the Reformation, which criticized the Catholic Church, when he posted his ninety-five theses on the door of the castle church in Wittenberg**
- **Hans Tausen (1494-1561), a former monk who had been a student of Luther's in Wittenberg, brought Lutheranism to Denmark**
- **Sociologists credit Denmark's brand of Lutheranism for building its "better model."**

Erika continued when Terri nodded ten minutes later.

"Here's the problem with Fukuyama's idea. A liberal democracy requires three conditions—a stable state, rule of law, and accountability for the three branches of government, which are the executive, legislative, and judicial. They might not be achievable in many parts of the world, but even if they are, Denmark might be a better model."

Erika paused for Terri to ponder her words; Terri spoke a minute later.

"I see where you're taking this. We can hold a town hall meeting in Copenhagen to make a video that shows me asking citizens what should be done to defend democracy against the accelerating rise of tyranny and authoritarianism. It'll be a video everyone will want to watch. I'm going to tell Fraser right now."

"Good, and while you're doing that, I'll work on my online courses. Let me know what the next step is."

Terri came back two hours later.

"Fraser says it's a go. He'll arrange a crew and audience for one town hall meeting in Copenhagen at 8 p.m. on Wednesday, February 20th. That gives you two weeks to prepare the script and questions. And he says not to worry; he'll give us everything we need, so getting to and from Denmark will be fun and safe."

"I'll be ready; in fact, I'll make you even more than ready by adding some ice-breakers you can use to build audience rapport before launching into the script and questions. You'll have them the day before we leave."

Thanks to practicing with Erika, Terri built empathy with the audience by needing no teleprompter, and they liked her spontaneous delivery when she started the meeting.

"I have researched enough to know why 'getting to Denmark' is a route many developing countries want to take. After all, this small country is the home of many great people. Hans Christian Andersen wrote Fairy Tales that are known around the world. You can even see a statue in the harbor of his most famous, *The Little Mermaid*. We also have Nobel Prize-winning physicist Niels Bohr, and Carl Nielsen, a great 20th-century symphonic composer. And now, let me outline what my interview questions will entail…"

Terri asked for comments five minutes later.

A young woman made the first.

"Unlike America's male-oriented gender bias, Denmark's high level of male-female equality fosters behavior that transcends the gender barriers set by less egalitarian societies. As a feminine culture, Danes have more flexible gender roles, which allows them to be more relaxed when considering romantic relationships. The absence of pressure to fulfill certain gender-based stereotypes fosters a liberal attitude toward sex, dating, and marriage. I expect you will detect this when you compare our answers to those you would get in America."

A young man made the second.

"Our culture not only talks about sex but also watches porn movies. Denmark's flexible gender roles allow for a wider acceptance of sexual experimentation. In fact, we were the first country to establish the right for same-sex couples to have registered partnerships."

"Thank you both for telling me some reasons why I might find differences when making comparisons. And now, to my questions…"

After the presentation ended, Erika took her position by staying in the background, letting audience members congratulate Terri while the crew packed up to take them back to the hotel. Once in the room, Erika offered her assessment.

"Your interviewing skills get better each time, which makes final cut editing easier and easier. And while we're in Copenhagen, I have an idea for another town hall topic. Would you like to hear what it is, or would you like more time to decompress?"

"Please tell me now."

"I came across an organization called the Consensus for Climate Change that's based at the University of Copenhagen. It's run by a leading climatologist named Bo Lundberg. Why not use your New York Times status to set up a meeting where you can describe the video you want to make, spotlighting the impact of climate change on Scandinavia and what his organization is doing to help the world deal with it?"

"That's a great idea. You think I should run it past Fraser?"

"No, just tell him you're working on another when you send him the final cut of the interview you just completed."

"OK, then what?"

I'll write your script and question list; Bo and his assistant will take us on a chopper tour to see firsthand what's going on, and it should include Norway's Global Seed Vault, housed in a sandstone mountain on Norway's Spitzbergen Island. It stores seeds from plants worldwide to provide security for food supply and ecosystems. There's even a backup vault, the Nordic Gene Bank, housed in an abandoned coal mine. You can impress him by describing what you now know about Denmark and the seed banks, but let him tell you the details."

"Instead of calling, why don't we go visit the university tomorrow?"

"Good idea. Now, let's rest for tomorrow."

While Erika and Terri were making their meeting plans, Indira was already listening to Electra.

"I am pleased to report that Erika continues to mature physically, emotionally, and cognitively. She has done this with Marilyn Tarrant's help and my guidance. I am monitoring her latest international adventures, from which I will guide her to additional projects that fit with yours."

"When will she be ready to learn more about her extraordinary legacy?"

"That will depend on her continued progress that I am monitoring."

"Excellent. Please proceed, as will I."

Indira's avatar left the screen.

CHAPTER 12

"The Doomsday Vaults"

MARCH 2228

While Terri talked with Bo on the charter flight to the seed vault, Erika listened to his assistant, Cuyler Pedersen, describe the terrain.

"Spitzbergen Island is 1550 miles from Copenhagen and only 500 miles from the North Pole. And we'll tell the pilot to fly along a fjord so you can see what passengers on the cruise ships see…"

Erika took in every word, which she compared with the view thirty minutes later.

Norway's magnificent fjords penetrate miles and miles inland along steep cliffs. No wonder fjord cruises are world-renowned but becoming increasingly restricted. Norway is the most eco-focused country in Scandinavia, and unlike Alaskan cruises, which feature wildlife and glaciers, the ones here emphasize the gorgeous panoramic landscape.

How lucky for me…sightseeing is a wonderful fringe benefit, as is meeting Cuyler…how different he is from most of the males Terri and I encounter back home…his Norwegian personality is refreshingly open and respectful of females...his Scandinavian features make him good looking too…maybe we can do more than sightsee when we get back to Copenhagen…

Erika followed behind Terri and Cuyler while a security guard took Bo and his retinue into the seed vault. Erika absorbed every word Bo spoke.

"This vault has storage capacity to last 300 years, and we can tunnel deeper when more space is required. We chose the location so the vault will be above sea level even if all glaciers and ice sheets melt, and it is below the permafrost line, which maintains a below-freezing temperature. That reduces the energy load for the cryogenic storage units. We also control the humidity, which is critical for preserving seeds.

"We have repurposed our seed vault several times since it opened in 2008. Today, it is much more than an international cryogenic safe deposit box. We test all samples when storing them, and we do research that we share with all nations storing samples. Other nations have seed vaults, like the one in Fort Collins, Colorado, but it, like many others, does research for food companies that develop genetically modified organisms."

Bo stopped to ask questions after the guard took them to a lower level. Erika waited until none came from anyone else.

"Do you store any animal DNA or reproductive cells?"

"Excellent question. No, we don't, but Fort Collins does for important livestock. But we store the greatest breadth and depth of plant species in case climate change destroys too much of the world's ecology. Will that answer satisfy you?"

"I guess so, but your vault is for a worst-case scenario. I might call it a doomsday vault."

"You are very incisive. Some videos give it the same label, but I prefer to be less gloomy. Well, now, let's proceed to our testing and research center…"

The four boarded the charter plane four hours later for the four-hour flight back to Copenhagen. Bo, Cuyler, and Terri used half the time to plan for another town hall meeting and would reconvene tomorrow morning to begin implementation. Meanwhile, Erika decompressed while listening to herself.

I now know enough to write a dandy interview script, question list, and first draft of Terri's voiceover. If I meditate until we land, I might be fresh enough to start tonight and continue tomorrow…and I'll make sure to save some time for Cuyler…

But a surprise greeted Erika when she logged in soon after midnight. Electra's always pert-looking avatar appeared.

"How nice that you were so alert and proactive during the seed vault tour. Your climate change town hall meeting should unfold nicely, but I have a suggestion for what you might like to add when wrapping up the voiceover. What do you think that might be?"

"Can you give me a clue?"

"I'll give you the big one–doomsday vault–which you figured out on the tour before anyone else. Now, connect it to animals."

Erika puzzled the clues for over a minute when a flash of insight burst.

"I think I see the connection. There might not be a vault for storing animal DNA or reproductive cells collected from around the globe. Maybe each major country has its own and jealously guards it. Is that it?"

"You're partway there. There are only two WHO-designated sites for storing dangerous bacteria and viruses, America's Centers for Disease Control in Atlanta and Russia's Center for Research on Virology and Biotechnology in Koltsovo, which don't cooperate. And given the troubled state of international politics, other adversarial nations have their own. You should call them doomsday vaults."

Electra waited for Erika to add more.

"And how about this? We could have a vault for extinct species and one for emerging life forms. The possibilities for progress and regress are immense."

"Excellent. You don't need to give all the ominous implications, but listeners might like a subtle warning you can place at the end of the voiceover."

"When should I share this with Terri?"

"Only when you give her your final voiceover for the final cut. Now, do some surfing to confirm the facts I've given you, then rest for tomorrow so you're ready to go. And by the way, I think you and Cuyler might enjoy some time together after work. Just use your common sense. And I'm ready to go too, so stay healthy and safe."

Electra's avatar departed.

The rest of Erika's stay in Copenhagen seemed almost like a vacation. Working with Terri was now second nature, and time with Cuyler was her best opposite-sex experience ever.

When returning to the London office a week later, Erika knew what to say when Terri asked her to help edit the video.

"I've already been working on it in my head. And I think you'll like the voiceover for the final cut. Pay special attention to your closing remarks."

"Thanks, and if that's the case, Spencer and Mrs. Walthers will love it. Who knows? Maybe it'll get us another promotion or travel assignment. But no matter what, our teamwork will make the best of whatever comes our way…"

CHAPTER 13

"An Unexpected Trip"

APRIL 2228

Fraser's emphatic tone accented the words he was speaking to Terri at the London office.

"No doubt about it. You've got the knack for picking topics and making town hall videos audiences everywhere love. That's why your next trip will be to Paris."

"When do we leave? And what are the details?"

"The last week of April, which gives you three weeks to prepare. The Times will collaborate with Le Monde, France's leading evening newspaper. Its academic, left-of-center point of view fits perfectly with ours."

Terri looked like she had more questions.

"Le Monde means the world, doesn't it? And you'll coordinate the crew, location, and audience size?"

"Don't fret about that. You can handle whatever Le Monde comes up with. Keep doing the scripting questioning, final cut video editing, and voiceover. I can't think of anything else you need to know for the time being, so please carry on."

Terri Emailed the facts to Erika, who was working at the apartment. Her reply said she'd begin working immediately.

Terri's excitement wouldn't fit in the kitchen, so she took Erika to a quiet local pub to discuss the assignment. Erika spoke as soon as they were sitting in a cozy booth.

"I've begun surfing for info about France that I'll put at the start of your script so you can show you've done your homework. We'll say that France should be fiercely proud of its continental philosophical, political, and literary accomplishments. And we can summarize the country's political framework, which is a parliamentary government composed of two chambers; the upper

Senate has 349 members, and the lower National Assembly has 577 coming from the nation's geographic districts."

"And I can add to that. France and Germany are the leading European nations. But what topics should we cover?"

"Let's cover two that are interrelated and compare what people in France say with those in the United States, focusing on democracy, economics, immigration, and concern about genetically modified organisms."

"You've got it all scoped out, but I can add a segue at the start that'll take us to the serious stuff. France is the world's culinary leader for cheese, croissants, and wine."

Erika warmed to the wordplay.

"And if we sample them when we get there, that'll add to our travel fringe benefits."

The duo made rapid progress by working independently during the day and collaborating at the apartment during the evening. Erika had just shown the latest draft of the script when Terri's cell phone rang. She stood from the couch and stretched her arms overhead before answering.

"This is Terri Tarrant…Who?…What?…" Terri dropped the phone before collapsing onto the couch, unable to speak.

Erika grabbed it and spoke.

"Hello, I'm Erika Kincaid, Terri's roommate. She just collapsed. What did you say to her?"

"This is the District of Columbia Medical Examiner's Office calling to inform Ms. Tarrant that her parents died in an automobile accident yesterday. She is the only living relative we could locate, and she must make a funeral or other arrangement to dispose of the corpses…Hello, are you still there?"

Erika spoke as soon as the shock subsided.

"Uh, yes. Would you please give me your name and phone number so we can call back once we know what Terri wants to do?"

After jotting the information and ending the call, Erika ran to the bathroom to get a washcloth and towel. Terri had just lost her lunch and dinner.

Terri finally spoke after Erika tidied her up.

"Did you hear that? It's, it's—" Erika shook her by the shoulders to help her focus.

"It's terrible news, but we have to deal with it. Think…what do you want to do?"

"I, I don't know. I thought they'd live forever, you know, that they'd always be around."

Terri ran out of words, so Erika took charge.

"OK, let's get you lying down; I'll figure out what we should do."

After helping Terri into bed, Erika took the only action she could think of. Electra's avatar appeared minutes later, wearing a serious expression and waiting for Erika to speak.

"Terri and I have a big, big problem. Her parents died in a DC auto accident yesterday. She doesn't know what to do, and I don't know either. Will you help us?"

Electra's tone and expression showed infinite empathy.

"Yes, I have dealt with these tragedies in previous lifetimes. Here are the steps I will coordinate. From what I already know, Mr. Tarrant had an important position in Washington. I will contact his office to follow up with his lawyer, who should know about a will, financial status, etc."

"How will you do that?'

"Please trust me. I have contacts, too. Invoke me tomorrow evening, and I will tell you what to do. And first thing tomorrow morning, tell Fraser about Terri's tragedy. You and Terri will need to make an unexpected trip to DC."

After Electra's avatar vanished, Erika pondered the enormity of what she and Terri faced. Electra set plans in motion by contacting Indira.

The whirlwind subsided by the time the girls caught a Saturday flight to Washington. Erika used the first couple of hours on the flight to brief Terri.

"According to your father's lawyer, you are your parent's closest living relative. Your grandparents died years ago, and you have no aunts or uncles. Do you know of any others?"

"There are None. What else did you find out?"

"Your parents died intestate, which means they do not have a will, so all their assets have to go through probate. Did you know your parents were over two million in debt? Your dad even took out a second mortgage on the house to pay for your mother's cancer treatments that weren't covered by healthcare."

"They never told me about any of this, and I was too self-centered to ask."

Terri stopped talking to wipe away tears, so Erika filled the silence.

"Did you bring a set of keys to your parent's house? We can stay there if you did."

Terri looked in her purse before nodding yes.

"Good. It'll be our base of operations. I've arranged for a closed-casket service at a funeral parlor in Chevy Chase. It will make all arrangements for posting an obituary in newspapers and then placing ashes a couple of days afterward in the burial vault your parents have."

Stopping when she saw Terri's emotions carrying her away, Erika hugged her, and then each withdrew into their separate spaces for the remainder of the flight.

Erika's thoughtful preparations helped keep Terri's emotions in check during the wake and ecumenical service. Afterward, she did some of the talking at a restaurant where Erika treated them to an early dinner.

"I never realized my father had so many powerful friends. Several of them told me I was fortunate to have such kind and loving parents. I hate myself for never telling them how much they meant to me, and now I never can. I'm now on my own."

Terri paused to calm her emotions before continuing.

"You're lucky; your parents are still alive. Why won't you introduce me to them? After all, we're like sisters."

"They're gone most of the time. And you're not alone. We have each other. Listen to the song 'Part of Me Part of You' to understand why."

"OK, but I still hate myself."

"Don't. Parents don't expect children to dote on them until much later in life. If you could talk to your mother, she would tell you to remember only once in a while all the good they did for you as you make the most of your life."

Erika could see Terri's resolve rise to the occasion.

"Then we better fly back to London. When do we leave?"

"Our return flight has an open date. I'll schedule it for the first Friday in May. That'll give you enough time to talk with the lawyer and close up the house while I get the Paris town hall script stuff finished."

"OK, let's do it. That'll get me moving again."

Erika checked her packing late in the afternoon on the departure date before checking in with Electra, whose pert expression appeared on her laptop as she spoke.

"You have helped your kindred sister regain her footing, which also helps you. What else have you learned on this trip?"

Erika had to think for a minute before answering.

"That close friends might become family, and young people won't understand the point of life until they're much older."

"How insightful you have become. Here is a poem called 'To the Point' I heard several lifetimes ago that expresses the same sentiments.

It's taken years to understand,
The focal point of Life.
But now I see its majesty,
No more internal strife.

When young we think that all is ours,
The world revolves round us.
And when our whims aren't fully met,
We make a terrible fuss.

But look beyond your selfish self,
For a selfless path that's right.
Reach out to those with heavy needs,
Help make their burden light.

Now get to the airport for your return flight. That will get both of you back in action."

Erika followed Electra's command.

CHAPTER 14

"Back in Action"

MAY 2228

Fraser seemed as pleased as Erika that Terri had regained her step, although she hid her feelings at his meeting the Monday they returned.

"Of course, you have our condolences, but keeping busy is perhaps the best way to deal with grief. I have rescheduled the Paris trip for the first week of June. You should have plenty of time to prepare a video or two that will air in July. All other details remain the same. If you can, connect your topics to France's major July holiday, Bastille Day, held on July 14th. So, unless you have questions, we shall adjourn the meeting."

Letting Terri reacquaint herself with work at the office, Erika left for their apartment. Once there, she logged on to review what she had already prepared.

I've made all the changes I need for video number one. I can rehearse Terri as soon as she's ready…and until then, I'll start thinking about topics for the second one until we leave for Paris…once there, I'll do my own daytime sightseeing to trigger the details…

Several days later, the duo departed for Paris. Upon arrival, they went to the Paris office of the Times for Terri to meet her crew and its coordinator, who would make all arrangements with the French newspaper Le Monde.

Erika saw enough to realize there was little she could do until Terri was ready to practice rehearsing for video number one, so she told Terri before returning to the hotel.

Erika played the role of a typical tourist for the next several mornings by taking bus tours to the most popular attractions. She started with the Eiffel Tower, then the Louvre Art Museum, and followed that with Notre Dame Cathedral, which is on an island in the center of the city.

She enjoyed listening to the guides, who answered an array of questions they must have heard thousands of times. She summarized some of the answers to herself.

Paris has been called 'The City of Lights' ever since becoming the first European city to illuminate its streets with gas lighting.

The Louvre Palace houses the Louvre National Art. Built in the late 13th century, it was originally a fortress, but as the city grew, it could no longer fulfill its defensive function.

In the mid-16th century, it became the residence of kings until Louis the Fourteenth, known as the Sun King, moved in 1682 to the Palace of Versailles. After that, it became a place to display the royal collection of art, and in 1692, the Royal Academy of Painting and Sculpture moved in.

The art museum opened in 1793 with an exhibition of nearly 500 paintings owned by previous kings or confiscated from the Church. And ever since, its collection has grown steadily despite the trials and tribulations of world politics.

Erika ended her third day of touring by visiting the world-famous shopping district on the Champs-Elysees Boulevard, which in Greek mythology means the field of paradise. It connects the Arc de Triomphe with the historic public square, Place de la Concorde, the execution site during the French Revolution.

The tours accomplished what Erika needed; she now knew the topic of the second video and wrote up the script, questions, and voiceover, but she wouldn't share them until Terri sent the final cut of the first video to Fraser and Mrs. Walthers.

Feeling so good about the final cut, Terri asked Erika to plan a few sightseeing days. She found a no-waiting special group tour that would take a thirty-minute train ride to the Palace and Gardens of Versailles for day one, then for day two, a walking tour of the most famous Parisian art community, Monmarte, perched atop a small hill in the eighteenth arrondissement–the French word for administrative district–which, according to the guide, has lost none of its village atmosphere that attracted so many artists of the 19th and 20th centuries.

Erika steered them from the crowded cafes to street vendors selling macarons served with coffee or wine, and she bought two each, filled with chocolate, pistachio, or banana.

Terri sounded happily relaxed at a café near the hotel Erika chose for dinner that evening.

"You really showed me France's rich history. You think we can find a topic to connect with it?"

"That's the plan. We'll outline French and American artistic cultures, focusing on painting, literature, and film, and then we'll ask the audience to compare them. Are the gaps narrowing, and what about when comparing to emerging third world art?"

"How will you summarize all that so it fits in the script?"

"I've scoped it out this way. France is the Guardian of Tradition, the Artistic Aristocrat. Its centuries-old heritage is full of elegance and sophistication.

"The United States is the Land of Reinvention, the Energetic Innovator, known for its can-do spirit, a place that nurtures dreams and ambitions.

"The French character seeks balance in life. It values leisure, work-life harmony, and extended vacations. The art of relaxation is foremost in the café culture along the Seine, where Parisians savor the moments.

"The American character relentlessly pursues success. It's a place that celebrates hard work, and ambition fuels the journey. The American dream is the hero's path, marked by a relentless pursuit of goals. How do you like that?"

"Maybe we can start by saying France and the U.S. have emerged as two distinct and wonderful countries having much to offer, and their differences make the world a more colorful and diverse place to explore. Then you can wordsmith what you just said into a segue for the questions."

"I'll give you the script and questions the day after tomorrow. Then you can practice with the crew while I work on the voiceover."

"Let's do it. At this rate, we can send the final cut to Fraser and Mrs. Walther in time for a London flight by the end of the month."

And they did. Terri asked the rhetorical question Erika expected on the ride to the airport.

"So, what should we pick for the next topic?"

"Let's go with what you already mentioned."

"I forgot what I said. Please tell me."

"France and Germany are the leading European countries. So, I'll find a topic if you set up a trip to Germany."

"And how about running the meeting in its capital, Berlin?"

 That's the best choice."

"Do you want to talk about it on the flight?"

"Not unless I feel better…"

The crush of people at the airport unsettled Erika's stomach. She pulled Terri to a halt when she spied what she needed.

"I have to go to the bathroom. You keep going; I'll meet you at the gate."

Erika waited for several waves of diarrhea to come and go, then washed her hands and face before heading to the gate. Once there, she sat next to Terri and stared around the lounge area while Terri read a magazine. But she panicked when the first boarding call sounded.

"Oh my god, I left my ticket in the restroom. You board, and I'll catch up."

Erika dashed to the restroom, accompanied by good luck. The attendant had found it. She pulled some dollar bills out of her purse and said merci while exchanging them for her ticket, then raced back in time to make the last boarding call.

Erika tried to settle down when the flight reached cruising altitude, but not even meditation helped. Terri spotted her discomfort.

"What's wrong?"

"My heart's pounding like it's about to come out of my chest. You better—" Erika collapsed forward before she could say more.

Terri pushed the call attendant button while screaming.

"Help, I've got a medical emergency."

Two flight attendants and a doctor on the flight came to her aid. They stretched Erika flat in the aisle, then gave her oxygen while monitoring her blood pressure and pulse.

Erika stirred five minutes later, and they helped her buckle in.

"We'll have a medical technician waiting at the gate. Have your friend drink water, and push the button again if you need further assistance."

"I will. Thanks for all you've done."

Erika's sense of humor came to life when the technician came to wheel her off the plane.

"This is the best excuse ever for being first off the plane."

Terri smiled for the first time since the flight began.

CHAPTER 15

"Ominous Warnings from the Fatherland"

JULY 2228

As soon as they landed, Terri took Erika to the A&E–the Accident and Emergency Center, which is London's version of America's ER–closest to their apartment.

Three hours later, they sat as the attending physician explained his diagnosis.

"I found nothing to suggest a serious heart condition, but it's possible her heart murmur might exacerbate an arterial blockage. Have a cardiologist do additional testing when she returns to the United States."

Erika felt good enough to speak for herself.

"So, can I get back to work tomorrow?"

"Yes, but resume action gradually and take aspirin twice a day."

Terri had heard enough.

"Thank you for your help. I'll pay with my credit card."

Erika said more when they were in the apartment.

"Don't tell anyone at the Times. I don't work for them, and as long as you keep churning out the videos, they don't care what I do."

"OK, tomorrow I'll tell Fraser you're doing some research for me on my next assignment, which will be a town hall meeting in Berlin. That'll keep him happy, but will you be OK working here?"

"Sure, I enjoy working independently. The pressure's off, and I can take a break from surfing whenever I want. You can organize for Berlin while I find a topic."

"You look tired. Let's go to bed."

In the days that followed, Erika dug into Germany's legacy, which she summarized to herself.

Germany has fully emerged from behind the cloud of World War II and last century's Russian confrontations to become Europe's economic and technological powerhouse, building on its unparalleled metaphysicians, starting with Kant, progressing through Hegel, Husserl, and Heidegger, and culminating in Schopenhauer, Nietzsche, and Freude.

It also has great classical and romantic composers…this combination alone makes Germany a country the world looks up to.

Erika took the weekend off before delving into the country's political views, which she summarized three days later.

Germany's energy policy is detrimental to nuclear and green energy because of its inefficient bureaucracy. How odd for a country whose expertise and efficiency make its businesses run like a digital clock.

Its government is a staunch defender of democracy and rightfully distrusts Russia because of centuries-long conflict, but unlike America, it has more faith in China…Germany is its biggest supplier.

I must research another piece to the topic, but not now… I need a break…

Noticing that Erika looked tired, Terri asked a delicate question when she came home that evening.

"I'm ready whenever you are to rehearse for our trip. When will you have the script and questions ready?"

"By Wednesday, if that's OK."

"That should be fine. I won't bother you this weekend. We can leave for Berlin sometime the week after next, and we won't do any sightseeing until after we complete the first video's final cut."

Erika started researching the last piece on Monday: Germany's technological intentions. By Wednesday, she had assembled the facts she would present to Terri that evening.

Terri sat transfixed by every word she said.

"I've already mentioned that Germany is focusing on economic growth, building out its infrastructure to collect Big Data, and pushing the envelope for A.I. development. However, it also wants to warn the world about risks similar to those in World War Two when Germany developed rockets and learned how to split the atom. Nevertheless, the government wants to become a global leader in artificial intelligence and is funding a national A.I. strategy implementation."

"But many countries have the same goal. What's different here?"

"Do you remember the blockbuster movie 'The Terminator?' It spawned a number of dystopian stories about a future world run by A.I. machines bent on exterminating humans. Germany worries the world is rushing into an accelerating A.I. arms race that holds risks far beyond those of drones or smart missiles. Super and smaller powers alike are already putting A.I.-empowered control software in their nuclear arsenals without knowing how the apps or failsafe systems will react if someone pushes the wrong button."

Erika paused for Terri, whose grimace said a lot.

"Did you find anything good to say?"

"It gets even worse. A.I. developers don't know what sort of ethics the control software has, and it can already make the kill decision, which takes humans out of the loop."

"So, what will you script for me to start the meeting?"

"Here's the outline; I'll compliment Germany for its outstanding heritage and current position on the world stage. Then I'll outline major current economic, political, and technological issues and write what I think the positions of the U.S. and German governments are. Then, you ask the questions to get the audience's comparisons. And then—" Terri's frustration showed when she interrupted.

"What about all that dystopian A.I. stuff?"

"I'll tone it down so you can wrap up with a mild warning about pushing A.I. too fast."

"OK. I don't want to think about this anymore until we get to Berlin. Maybe my optimism will show up…"

Terri's optimism returned as soon as she met her coordinator, who greeted her upon entering the offices of the Berliner Zeitung newspaper, Germany's equivalent of The Washington Post. His efficiency exceeded what she had experienced on all other trips and had her rehearsing with a video crew that afternoon. Erika stayed long enough to realize Terri didn't need her help, so she walked to the hotel, enjoying the local scene.

Clean streets, orderly Berliners walking about, and smooth-flowing trams and double-decker busses make the city look better than most capitals. Electric scooters and rent-a-bikes add to the modern feel. Maybe some sightseeing will stimulate topics for another video.

When Terri sent the final cut of video number one to Fraser and Mrs. Walther during the last week of July, Erika didn't have a second video topic, so she asked Terri for help.

"Ask your coordinator for some sightseeing places that connect with modern technological stuff, like power plants, airbases, and military installations. That would make for a good video topic. We can rent a car and visit them along with the typical sightseeing places, too."

"Couldn't that be risky?"

"That's why we'll ask your coordinator. He'll know the interesting but safe places to visit."

"This has possibilities. I'm told that Germans drive aggressively, but at least they drive on the right, so how about I drive and you navigate?"

"That's another way we make a great team. And in addition to keeping track of where we are, I'll get what we need to keep us safe. I learned that from you."

"Well, if you learned it from me, I guess it works. We're still moving. And between the two of us, we'll keep it that way…"

CHAPTER 16

"The Escape of the Transcendental Spies"

AUGUST 2228

Erika picked several traditional tourist attractions in Berlin to practice their driving and navigating coordination. The Berlin Wall and Checkpoint Charlie Memorial made a good start, followed by a visit to the Market-Hall Nine for a selection of German food and beer.

The next day included the Brandenburg Gate and the iconic Berlin TV Tower, which made an appropriate segue to high-tech sights outside of Berlin. Erika added one of her own, visiting an automated dyke system for flood control along the Rhine. Getting there required driving on Germany's storied autobahns, which have no speed limits, only recommendations.

Other than when on the autobahns, they kept a leisurely pace, which allowed for occasional stops at quaint towns, but at the end of a week, Erika still had nothing specific for building a script and told Terri they should change their plans.

"I think we should visit another country. Maybe Italy or Spain will spark a video topic. We should head back to our Berlin hotel and make plans to fly back to London this weekend. Fraser should be happy to see us because you told me he loves our latest video."

"OK, we'll fly back Sunday evening. What do you want to do before then?"

"Send our luggage ahead and then drive around so we get to the Brandenburg airport in time for our flight."

"Not a problem…"

Before making a prediction, Terri glanced through the windshield after she and Erika dashed to their rental car parked in their hotel's parking lot.

"I'm glad we did all our outdoor sightseeing when the sun shone. This evening's rain would spoil any we'd want to do on the drive to the airport, but it shouldn't make the drive too dangerous if lights stay on and drivers use a lighter foot on the pedal."

"It won't bother me either. Weather doesn't interfere with my cell phone's GPS location tracking unless it knocks down too many cell towers, and I don't think that's in the forecast."

As Terri pulled out of the parking lot and followed directions, Erika listened to Terri's rambling comments but couldn't comment. Cell phone tracking needed her undivided attention.

"I've been thinking…maybe you should work for the Times…maybe we should live permanently in London…maybe we should hold biotech town halls…maybe we should set up trips to Zimbabwe and India…if analysts are right and they merge into the next superpower, we can scoop the competition…I'll run that one past Fraser when we get to home base…"

According to Erika's tracking, she could see two dots on her cell phone, one moving, showing their car cruising on Autobahn A-113 toward a stationary one representing Brandenburg Airport, which is fifteen miles south of Berlin's center. She was about to tell Terry they would arrive in about fifteen minutes when suddenly, her cell's screen refreshed, now showing a second moving dot, and before she could push any button, a text message appeared.

"Electra says Bad Guys closing in. Do you copy? Over."

Stunned, Erika could do nothing but text back.

"I copy. Now what? Over."

"Follow my commands and don't ask questions. Over."

"Copy that. Over."

Terri didn't question directions for exiting A-113 until Erika told her to park in a convenience store parking lot, but another message told her what to say.

"I want to get a candy bar. I'll be back in a jiff." Erika grabbed her purse and dodged raindrops before running into the store and waiting for additional commands.

When the moving dot stopped next to Terri's car, another message came.

"Be ready to use what's in your purse and do what I command. Over."

"Roger that. Over."

Electra sent enough information in the next five minutes for Erika to follow Electra's action plan when the "Go" command came.

"Roger that. Over."

Clutching her purse, Erika raced through the rain and darkness to the Bad Guy's car, a police car with lights blazing. She pulled a gun and Bang-Bang blasted two bullets into the driver's side door window. The guy at the wheel gaped. So did the guy in the back seat who was interrogating Terri.

Erika screamed instructions.

"Both of you, drop your weapons slowly, get out of the car, and walk away." When the guy in back made too sudden a move, Erika put a bullet in his kneecap before giving another set of commands.

"Terri, grab his gun, push him out, and get your purse before getting behind the wheel. The guy in the front will be gone when you get back."

Two minutes later, Erika yelled another command while sitting next to Terri.

"Follow my directions and drive like hell."

Terri didn't have time to say anything. Keeping the car from skidding took all her concentration, as did Erika's for reading GPS tracking and Electra's text messages.

There was now one moving dot and one stationary. As their moving dot moved toward the stationary one, Erika knew it must be a safe haven but said nothing. And when a second moving dot appeared, Erika yelled directions meant to keep them away from the pursuing dot, telling Terri to speed up as the distance between kept shrinking.

Erika felt like a surreal video game player who had to get to the destination dot before the pursuing dot crashed into hers. The swerving and turning became fast and furious as the three dots came together.

Erika's last command came just in time.

"Blast through the gate."

Terri did and then slammed on the brakes just in time to keep from ramming into a guardhouse sign that read:

"United States Embassy."

Two men with guns drawn came running.

Erika knew what to say.

CHAPTER 17

"The Transcendental Revelation"

AUGUST 2228

Fraser made Terri tell her story twice before giving his opinion.

"So, you're telling me the BND wants to charge you with espionage because you seemed suspicious while sightseeing?"

"That's what they said, and they were very methodical. They spoke in clipped English when showing me their IDs, which spelled out Bundesnachrichtendienst above their photos, and they said they worked for Germany's foreign intelligence service. They didn't come out and say it, but I think they wanted to accuse me of spying."

"And then, your partner got the drop on them, and you commandeered their car and raced to the U.S. Embassy before another pursuit car could catch you?"

"That's it."

Fraser waited long enough to know that neither Terri nor Erika would say more.

"We better keep a lid on this. Otherwise, you'll show up in some media interview that could make you a target when on other international assignments. We better fly you back pronto to headquarters in New York and let Mrs. Walthers decide what's next. I'll arrange for your flight. Meanwhile, rest at your apartment until you depart."

Mrs. Walthers met with the duo for an hour mid-morning on Wednesday, the thirteenth, to confirm all she had heard from Fraser before telling them what might be next.

"You've outgrown your assignment in London. Erika, we'll pay for your online courses if you want to work for us by reporting to Terri. Both of you, please come back in a week. By then, I should have something you'll like. Until then, just relax."

The girls returned to Erika's house, but they couldn't relax until a cardiologist examined Erika. Two days later, he gave them the news.

"You have a blocked coronary artery that I can correct using a new, less-invasive procedure that inserts a drug-coated balloon stent. According to our tests, your blood type is AB negative, which is the rarest. Your friend, Terri, is type O negative, which is a donor type for you. If you decide to have the procedure, she can provide what we need to proceed."

Erika looked at Terri before speaking.

"Thank you, doctor. Please give me a couple of days to think about it."

The team went home for supper. Terri did most of the talking and wrapped up the conversation by saying,

"So many revelations have just hit us. What do you think we should do?"

"I have to think more before I know. I'm beat; I'm going to log on at my workstation and see if something comes to mind. See you later."

Erika had surfed aimlessly for an hour when suddenly, Electra's avatar appeared and spoke first.

"You have many options, but before you choose, remember the biblical quote from Luke 12:48: "From everyone who has been given much, much will be demanded; and from the one who has been entrusted with much, much more will be asked."

Electra waited for Erika, who now looked puzzled.

"So what? What does all this mean for me?"

"That you are ready to know who you are and what legacy you have received from the lightning brain."

"What? What's the lightning brain?"

"Please settle down, sit still, and pay attention to me..."

THE END

www.ingramcontent.com/pod-product-compliance
Lightning Source LLC
Chambersburg PA
CBHW020120310726
48970CB00002B/725